Sam Is My Sister

Ashley Rhodes-Courter   illustrated by MacKenzie Haley

Albert Whitman & Company
Chicago, Illinois

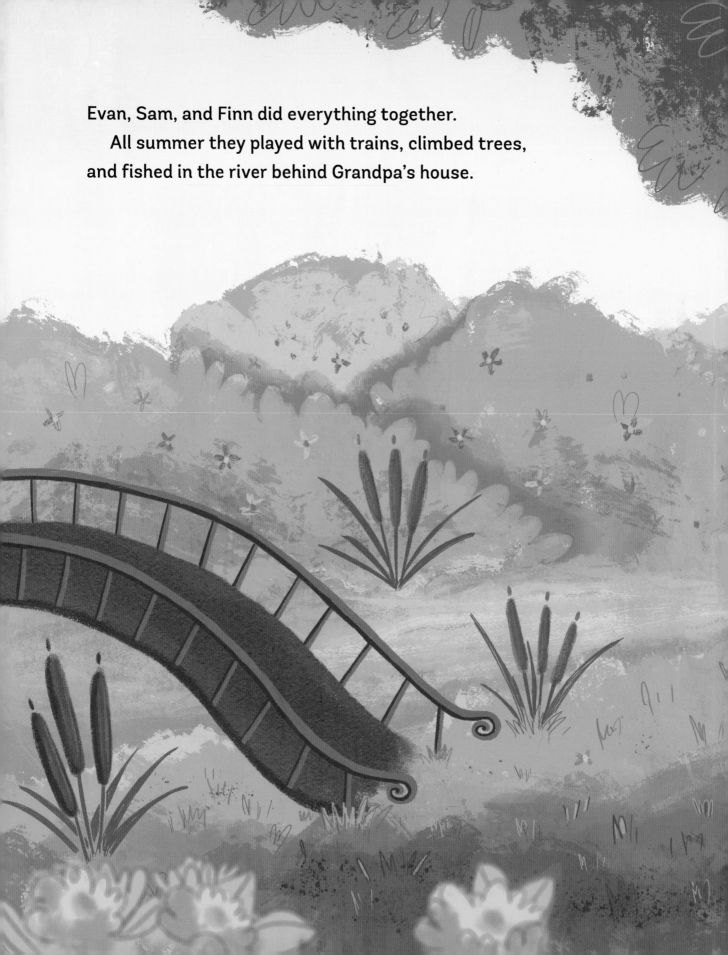

Evan, Sam, and Finn did everything together. All summer they played with trains, climbed trees, and fished in the river behind Grandpa's house.

They even went to outer space. Evan thought Sam and Finn were the perfect copilots.

"Five! Four! Three! Two! One!"
"Blast off!"
"Zoom! Zoom! Brothers to the moon!" Evan cheered.

At the library, they lugged books about space to the checkout desk.

"Wait!" Sam shouted before running back to the shelves.

Sam returned with a glittery book that had a long-haired princess on the cover.

"Why do you want a *girl* book instead of a space book?" Evan asked.

"Books are for everyone to enjoy," Mom said.

"And girls can go to space too!" Sam chimed in.

"Did you know doughnuts float in space?" Finn asked.

They all laughed. But Evan still wondered why Sam wanted that book.

It was time to get haircuts for school.

Evan and Finn got theirs cut shorter, like Dad's. Then it was Sam's turn.

"You're going to look so handsome!" Dad said.

"I don't want to look handsome!" Sam cried. "I want to be beautiful with long hair down to my toes!"

Mom and Dad looked at each other, and Mom shrugged.
"Just a trim for Sam," Dad told the barber.

"Why doesn't Sam want to look like us anymore?" Evan whispered to Dad.

"Well, buddy, its Sam's hair," Dad said. "A new hairstyle isn't hurting anyone."

Evan didn't understand, but he saw the huge
smile on Sam's face.

On the first day of school, Evan put on his
new clothes and showed Mom.
But Sam wasn't ready. "I don't like shorts.
I want to wear a dress."

"Dresses are for girls," Evan said. "Why do you want to dress all wrong?"

"I want to wear what I like," Sam said.

Mom seemed to be thinking. She left the room a moment and came back with a white hair bow.

"How about this for now?" Mom clipped the bow in Sam's hair.

Sam beamed. "It's perfect!"

At school, some older kids pointed and laughed at Sam. One tried to grab Sam's bow.

"Why are you wearing that?" he asked.

"Because I like it," Sam said.

"Boys don't put stuff in their hair," another boy added.

"Well, I do!" Sam shouted, and marched off.

Evan glared at the boys before running after Sam.

"Do you want to play spaceship?" Evan asked.
"Paging Commander Sam..." But Sam stayed quiet.
Evan tried again. "Zoom! Zoom! Brothers to—"
"I don't feel like playing," Sam said softly.

The morning bell rang.

"Line up," a teacher called. "Girls in one line, boys in another."

"Ms. Carson, where do I go?" Sam asked.

Evan wondered why Sam didn't get in line next to him and the other boys.

Ms. Carson looked over at Sam. "How about you just walk next to me," she said.

Mom and Dad started letting Sam wear dresses after school
and on the weekends. Sam couldn't wait to change into skirts
with bright tights, and put on pretty shoes.
    Evan had never seen Sam so happy.

"Why do you want to look like a girl?" Evan asked one day.

"Because I *am* a girl," Sam said. "On the inside." Sam drew a heart with a sparkly crayon.

"I don't get it," Evan replied. He picked up a crayon and drew a moon next to Sam's heart.

"So, how do you know which hand to use when you color?" Sam asked.

Evan stopped drawing for a moment. "I don't know. Drawing with my other hand doesn't feel right."

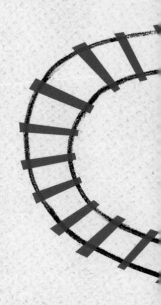

"Well, being a boy doesn't feel right to me," Sam explained. "It's just who I am."

Evan tried to draw a star with his other hand and got frustrated.

"This is weird. I'm glad no one makes me do this all the time," Evan said.

"Sam has been talking to us about something important," Mom said that night. "And Dad and I have met with some doctors and experts. We learned that for some people, the way they think and feel inside doesn't match what they look like on the outside. Even though Sam was called a boy at birth, Sam identifies as a girl. The word for that is transgender."

"Yes, that's me!" said Sam. "I want to be myself all the time."

Dad smiled at Sam. "You are in charge of who you are and how you feel."

"And we are in charge of making sure you kids are happy and healthy," Mom added.

"Well, *I* want to be in charge of dessert tonight!" Finn said.

"If you're a girl, can we still go fishing?" Finn asked.

"Of course we can!" Sam said.

"Girls like to fish, too, you know," Evan told Finn.

"What about playing spaceships, planes, and trains?" Finn wondered.

Sam laughed. "We can play anything, and with any toys!"

"We better tell Mom we're going to need a bigger toy box," Finn said.

At school, things weren't as easy.

"Sam, you can't play with us, because you're not a boy anymore," one boy said.

"No, that's just a boy in a dress," said a girl.

Evan got angry. "Hey, don't talk like that to my sister!"
He stood next to Sam until the mean kids walked away.

"You called me your sister," Sam said with a grin.
"Well, you are." Evan nodded.

Evan knew that Sam was still the same Sam.

That night at bedtime, Evan, Sam, and Finn watched as the moon rose and the stars sparkled through the clouds.

"What about going to the moon?" Finn whispered.

"Will you still want to come with us?" Evan asked.

"Princesses can go to the moon," Sam whispered back.

"Yes, they can," Evan said. "Zoom! Zoom! Family to the moon!"

Author's Note

This book is based on true experiences. Sam, Evan, and Finn (whose names have been changed) are my three children. They consented to sharing our story and were an integral part of the writing process.

My husband, Erick, and I served as foster parents for five years and have cared for more than twenty-five children. Sam, who was assigned male at birth, was placed in our home as a baby shortly before our son Evan was born. About a year later we were able to adopt Sam, and not long afterward we discovered I was pregnant with Finn.

Toddler Sam was drawn to princesses, purple, pink, and loved all things sparkly. During pretend play, Sam would always choose to be "Mommy" or "Sister." We didn't think much of this, as we believe kids should be free to explore their imaginations and play with whatever toys they like. In preschool, Sam's preferences for books and toys traditionally associated with girls became more consistent, insistent, and persistent than ever. Even Sam's teachers felt this was not a phase. By kindergarten, Sam was adamant about what she wanted to wear, what she wanted to be called, and how she wanted to be seen in the world.

As gender variance is discussed more in mainstream culture, children are finding their voices much sooner than in previous generations. One day, when we read aloud a wonderful book about a young transgender girl, Sam's face lit up. "Mommy, that's ME! I'm transgender!" This was a breakthrough moment. I had never seen Sam so happy.

Being both a clinical social worker and passionate mother, I dove into research and consulted many experts to find out how to best support Sam. Evan and Finn didn't fully understand why Sam wanted dresses and long hair—but they were able to put their love for Sam first. When Sam was called "she" or "her" at home or in public, she beamed. Her shift in mood and disposition was palpable and undeniable to family and Sam's teachers.